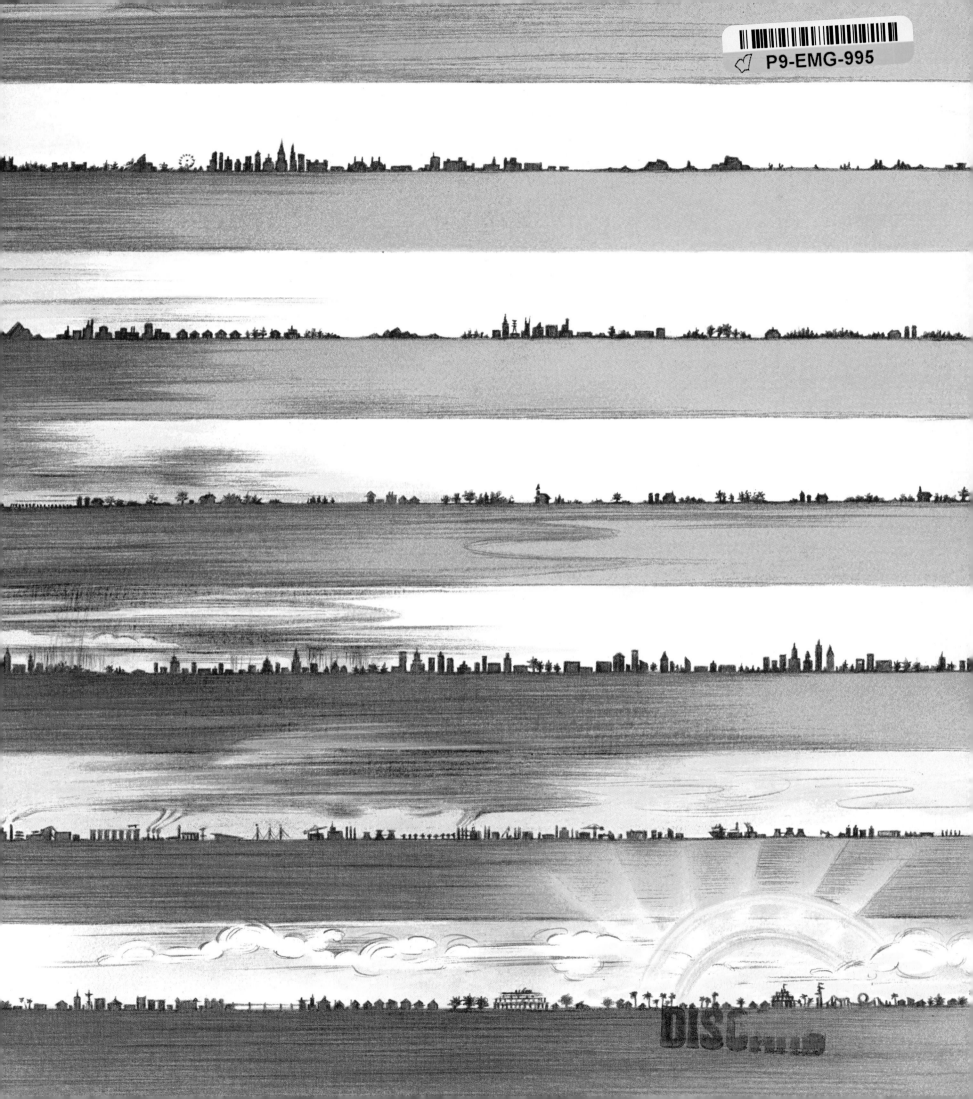

HILLARY RODHAM CLINTON

It Takes a Village

illustrated by
MARLA FRAZEE

Simon & Schuster Books for Young Readers • New York • London • Toronto • Sydney • New Delhi

Sometimes it takes a child

to make
a village.

We all have a place in the village, a job to do,

and a lot to learn.

Kids don't come with instructions.

But neither do grown-ups!

Every child needs a champion.

Or two.

Or three.

Or more.

And the right tool
to get the job done.

Every family needs help sometimes.

Kindness

and caring

and sharing

matter.

Playing matters too.

And resting.

Because the world is in a hurry,

but
children
are
not.

The village needs every one of us to help
and every one of us to believe in each other.

Children are
born believers.
And citizens, too.

Let us build a village . . .

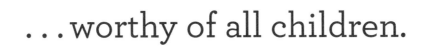

...worthy of all children.

AUTHOR'S NOTE

The old African proverb "It takes a village to raise a child" is a timeless reminder that children will only thrive if their families thrive. And in today's world that includes all kinds of families raising and loving children. We live in an interdependent world, where what our children hear, see, feel, and learn affects how they grow up and who they turn out to be. I believed this as a mother and even more strongly now as a grandmother. I have two reinforcing beliefs about this: Parents are the most important influences on their children, and no family, even the most privileged, exists in a vacuum. That's why I've worked hard over the years to help support families with good jobs, affordable child and health care, and effective public schools, as well as safe communities, clean air and water, and healthy food. All of us—from teachers to doctors to neighbors to employers to police and politicians—have to step up to support our villages.

Science has proven how resilient children can be despite great obstacles. And how creative and productive they can be starting at young ages. I'm inspired by the children and young people I've met over the years. And this book is meant to spark a conversation with our youngest about what children can do to help make the world what they hope it will be. The task illustrated by the extraordinary Marla Frazee is building a playground, but it could be donating food to a homeless shelter or cleaning up a park or speaking out against prejudice, all of which I've seen children do.

Now more than ever we need to support children and families. And when the news is grim or the odds seem long, look into the faces of children you know, and imagine what kind of country and world awaits them. I love being around children and reading to them and listening to the stories they tell us. That's especially true when it comes to my grandchildren, Charlotte and Aidan, whose lives and futures live in my heart.

The simple message of *It Takes a Village* is as relevant as ever: We are all in this together. I hope you enjoy sharing this book with the children in your life.

For Charlotte and Aidan
—H. R. C.

For Hillary, from one of the grateful villagers
—M. F.

SIMON & SCHUSTER BOOKS FOR YOUNG READERS
An imprint of Simon & Schuster Children's Publishing Division
1230 Avenue of the Americas, New York, New York 10020
Text copyright © 2017 by Hillary Rodham Clinton
Illustrations copyright © 2017 by Marla Frazee
All rights reserved, including the right of reproduction in whole or in part in any form.
SIMON & SCHUSTER BOOKS FOR YOUNG READERS is a trademark of Simon & Schuster, Inc.
For information about special discounts for bulk purchases, please contact
Simon & Schuster Special Sales at 1-866-506-1949 or business@simonandschuster.com.
The Simon & Schuster Speakers Bureau can bring authors to your live event. For more information
or to book an event, contact the Simon & Schuster Speakers Bureau at
1-866-248-3049 or visit our website at www.simonspeakers.com.
Book design by Marla Frazee and Ann Bobco
The text for this book was set in Archer.
The illustrations for this book were done in pencil and watercolor on Strathmore paper.
Manufactured in the United States of America
0817 LAK
First Edition
2 4 6 8 10 9 7 5 3 1
CIP data for this book is available from the Library of Congress.
ISBN 978-1-4814-3087-6
ISBN 978-1-4814-3088-3 (eBook)